# UNDER THE FAIRY TALE TREE

## A Whole-Language Approach To Teaching Thinking Skills

HANSEL AND GRETEL

JACK AND THE BEANSTALK

THE SLEEPING BEAUTY

CINDERELLA

JORINDA AND JORINGEL

RUMPELSTILTSKIN

THE LITTLE MATCH GIRL

THE PRINCESS AND THE PEA

RED RIDING HOOD

SNOW WHITE AND THE SEVEN DWARFS

**Educational Impressions**

Written by Vowery Dodd Carlile
Illustrated by Karen Neulinger

ISBN 1-56644-957-X

# Contents

# FOREWORD

Children around the world enjoy fairy tales. *Under the Fairy Tale Tree: A Whole-Language Approach to Teaching Thinking Skills* presents ten popular fairy tales which are used to teach critical and creative thinking skills. Each unit begins with a summary of the story and questions from Bloom's *Taxonomy.*\* Following these questions are independent project ideas developed to encourage creative thinking and writing.

The units may be used in any order. Begin each by reading the fairy tale to the class. (Although I have included summaries of the tales for your convenience, it is much preferable that you read to the children the detailed, illustrated, versions of the stories.) Ask any or all Bloom questions based upon the story. Then choose some or all of the projects for the students to complete.

After all the fairy tales have been read, play the game "Fairy Tale Magic." This game asks questions about all the fairy tales included in the book and provides a fun way to review and end the unit.

This has been my favorite book to write. I grew up loving fairy tales and still do. I hope this book will encourage your youngsters never to "outgrow" fairy tales!

I would like to thank my husband, Gene, and my children—Coleen, Casie, Corey and Pat—for their encouragement and support.

**Vowery Dodd Carlile**

\* Benjamin Bloom, *Taxonomy of Educational Objectives,* (New York: David McKay Company, Inc., 1956).

# INTRODUCTION

*Under the Fairy Tale Tree: A Whole-Language Approach to Teaching Thinking Skills* uses favorite fairy tales to teach children to read, think, and write critically and creatively. An important part of each unit is the series of questions and activities based upon Bloom's *Taxonomy of Educational Objectives.** Bloom divided cognitive development into six main levels: knowledge, comprehension, application, analysis, synthesis, and evaluation. Most of the questions presented to students fall into the first two categories, knowledge and comprehension. The highest levels are seldom used; they are more difficult to write and, because they have no definite answer, are more difficult to evaluate. The following is a brief description of the cognitive levels according to Bloom's taxonomy.

**Knowledge:** This level involves the **simple recall** of facts stated directly.

**Comprehension:** The student must **understand** what has been read at this level. It will not be stated directly.

**Application:** The student uses knowledge that has been learned and **applies** it to a new situation. He/She must understand that knowledge in order to use it.

**Analysis:** The student **breaks down** learned knowledge into small parts and analyzes it. He/She will pick out unique characteristics and compare them with other ideas.

**Synthesis:** The student can now **create** something new and original from the acquired knowledge. This level involves a great deal of creativity.

**Evaluation:** The student makes a **judgment** and must be able to back up that judgment.

* Benjamin Bloom, *Taxonomy of Educational Objectives,* (New York: David McKay Company, Inc., 1956).

The shape activities are another integral part of each unit. They are designed to promote higher-level creative-thinking skills. These activities can be used as class or independent projects.

Independent projects can be written to cover any subject using verbs that encourage responses from each of the six categories. Verbs for each of the categories include the following:

**Knowledge:** list, know, define, relate, repeat, recall, specify, tell, name

**Comprehension:** recognize, restate, explain, describe, summarize, express, review, discuss, identify, locate, report, retell

**Application:** demonstrate, interview, simulate, dramatize, experiment, show, use, employ, operate, exhibit, apply, calculate, solve, illustrate

**Analysis:** compare, examine, categorize, group, test, inventory, probe, analyze, discover, arrange, scrutinize, organize, contrast, classify, survey

**Synthesis:** plan, develop, invent, predict, propose, produce, arrange, formulate, construct, incorporate, originate, create, prepare, design, set up

**Evaluation:** conclude, value, recommend, evaluate, criticize, estimate, decide, value, predict, judge, compare, rate, measure, select, infer

These verbs can be used to design independent projects as well as to write your own higher-level questions in any subject area. Below is an example of the chart that I use when creating the independent projects in my books. I have also included a copy for you to reproduce and use when designing your own projects.

| CATEGORY | VERB | TOPIC | PROJECT |
|----------|------|-------|---------|
| Synthesis | Create | Cinderella | A story of Cinderella's life after she married the prince. |

By incorporating these question-and-project strategies into the curriculum, every child will be given the opportunity to be a creative thinker.

# Independent Projects Chart

| CATEGORY | VERB | TOPIC | PROJECT |
|----------|------|-------|---------|
|          |      |       |         |
|          |      |       |         |
|          |      |       |         |
|          |      |       |         |
|          |      |       |         |
|          |      |       |         |

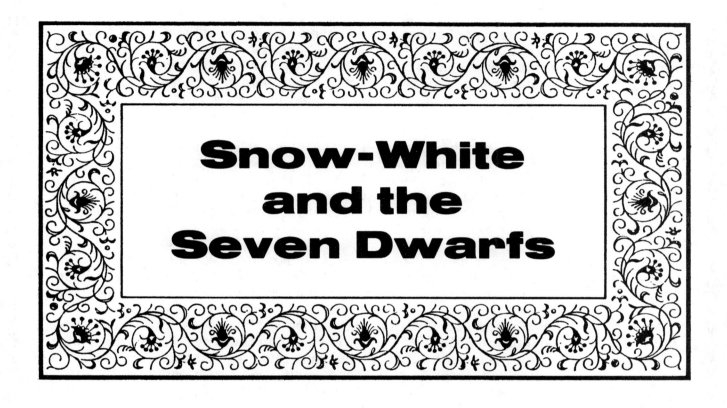

# Snow-White
# and the
# Seven Dwarfs

# Snow-White and the Seven Dwarfs

by the Brothers Grimm

## STORY SUMMARY

Once upon a time a queen pricked her finger as she embroidered at her window. Onto the pure white snow below fell three drops of blood. "Oh, that I had a child as white as snow, as red as blood, and as black as the wood of the embroidery frame," thought the queen. A short time later her wish came true, and a beautiful baby girl was born to the queen. The child had hair as black as the ebony of the frame, skin as white as snow, and lips as red as blood; she was named Snow-White.

When Snow-White was born, the queen died and about a year later the king remarried. The new queen was very envious. Often she gazed into her magic looking glass and asked, "Looking glass upon the wall, who is fairest of us all?" Usually, the mirror answered, "You are fairest of them all." But by the time Snow-White was seven, she had grown more beautiful than the queen, and the mirror answered, "Queen, you are full fair, 'tis true, but Snow-White fairer is than you."

The queen's envy turned to hatred; she ordered a huntsman to take Snow-White into the woods and kill her. But the huntsman took pity on the child and killed a wild boar instead. He took out the boar's heart and gave it to the queen as proof that he had killed the child.

Meanwhile, Snow-White wandered further and further into the woods. Finally, she came to a little house and took refuge in it. The house belonged to seven dwarfs, who were filled with joy when they saw the beautiful child. Snow-White told them her story, and they were happy to have her stay with them. In return, she would keep house and cook for them. Whenever they left her alone, they warned her never to open the door for anyone, for they knew that soon the queen would learn the truth.

When the queen found out that Snow-White was still alive, she went into the woods disguised as an old woman. First she tricked Snow-White into letting her lace her bodice so tightly that she could not breathe; however, the dwarfs came in time and loosened it. Next she tricked her into putting a poisonous comb in her hair, but the dwarfs saw the comb in time and removed it. The third time she tricked her into eating a poison apple. This time, however, the dwarfs could not figure out what was wrong.

Believing her dead but not having the heart to bury her, the dwarfs put Snow-White in a coffin of glass. One day a prince saw Snow-White and fell in love with her. He begged the dwarfs to let him take the coffin, and they agreed. As the prince's servants carried the coffin, the piece of poison apple that had lodged in Snow-White's throat came loose, and Snow-White came to life. The prince asked Snow-White to be his bride, and she accepted.

The wicked queen was invited to the wedding. There she was made to dance in red-hot shoes until she died.

Note: You may also wish to read the Disney version of the story to the children and have them compare and contrast the two.

# Questions & Activities Based Upon Bloom's Taxonomy

*Snow-White and the Seven Dwarfs*

**Knowledge:**
1. What fell on the white snow?
2. Who was supposed to kill Snow-White?
3. What was to be brought to the queen as proof that Snow-White had been killed?

**Comprehension:**
1. Why didn't Snow-White's stepmother like her?
2. What was Snow White to do in return for living in the dwarfs' home?
3. Explain how the stepmother fooled Snow-White.

**Application:**
1. What could Snow-White's stepmother have done to get rid of her instead of having her killed?
2. The queen had a problem with Snow-White. Think of a problem you have had. How did you solve your problem?
3. How might you have treated Snow-White if she had been your stepdaughter?

**Analysis:**
1. How was Snow-White's real mother different from her stepmother?
2. Compare the Seven Dwarfs with the huntsman.
3. How do you think Snow-White felt when left alone in the woods? How would you feel?

**Synthesis:**
1. How would the story have been different had the dwarfs not agreed to give the prince the coffin?
2. What would have happened if Snow-White had not awakened?
3. If you were the huntsman, how might you trick the queen into believing that Snow-White was dead?

**Evaluation:**
1. Was it right for Snow-White's stepmother to be so jealous of her? Why or why not?
2. Do you think Snow-White and the prince will be happy together? Why or why not?
3. Could this story really have happened? Explain.

**Create a secret hideaway for Snow-White in the forest. Draw a picture of your hideaway on another sheet of paper.**

## Draw a map that shows the prince how to find Snow-White.

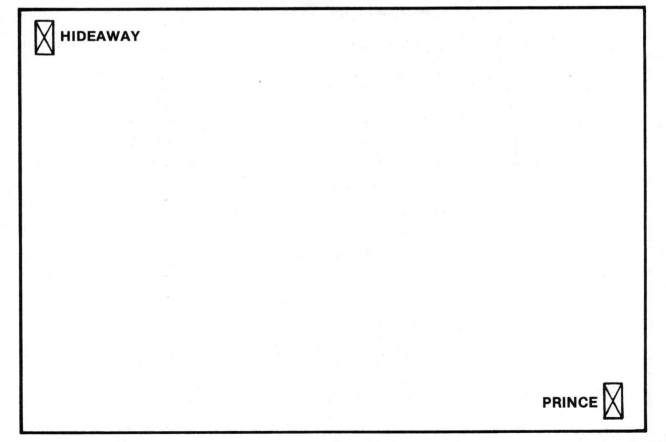

⊠ HIDEAWAY

PRINCE ⊠

Design a diary in which Snow-White might write down her thoughts and feelings.

## Draw your cover design here.

## Design your inside pages here.

5

**Plan a crossword puzzle based upon the story. Try it out on your friends.**

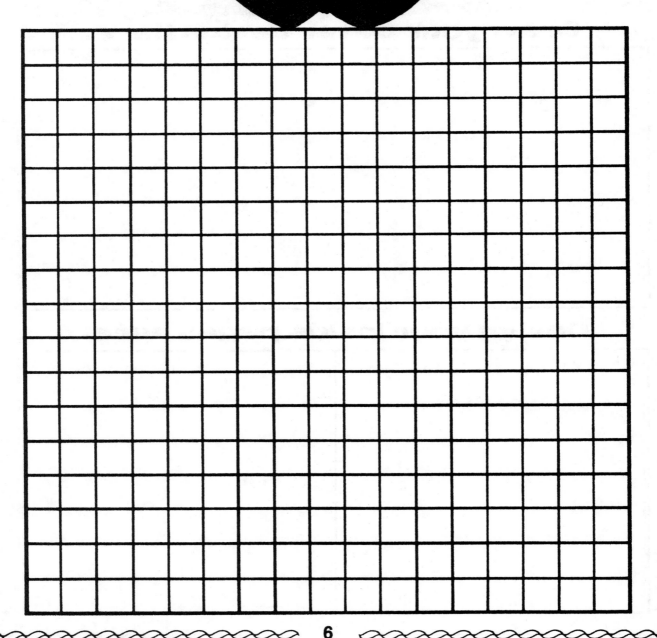

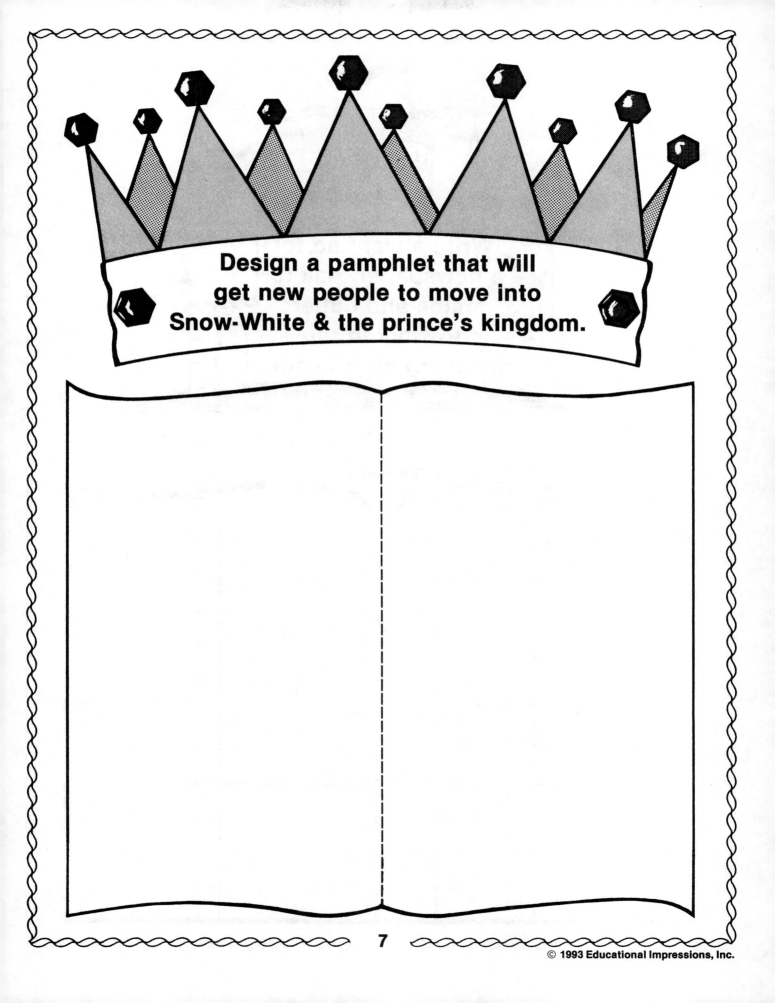

**Design a pamphlet that will get new people to move into Snow-White & the prince's kingdom.**

**Write a want ad for a newspaper. Ask for maids and butlers to work in the royal couple's castle.**

HELP WANTED

# The Sleeping Beauty

# The Sleeping Beauty

by Charles Perrault

## STORY SUMMARY

Once upon a time a king and queen ordered a great banquet to be held in celebration of their daughter's christening. To the banquet they invited seven fairies, but they neglected to invite the eighth fairy, whom they believed had died. Unfortunately, the wicked old fairy found out about the banquet and came anyway. Although the king ordered that a place be set for her, the eighth fairy was still displeased because there was a beautiful gift for each of the other fairies but not for her.

When the banquet ended, each of the fairies prepared to bestow her special gift upon the child. Fearing what the wicked old fairy might do, however, the youngest fairy hid behind a curtain and listened. The first six fairies bestowed upon the princess intelligence, beauty, kindness, generosity, gaiety and grace. (In some versions the gifts are beauty, the temper of an angel, grace, perfection in dancing, the ability to sing like a nightingale and the ability to play a musical instrument.) Then the old fairy proclaimed her gift: when the child is about 16, she will prick her finger with the spindle of a spinning wheel and die. Luckily, the youngest fairy still had a gift to bestow. Although she couldn't completely reverse the old fairy's spell, she could change it so that the princess would not really die, but merely sleep for 100 years until awakened by a prince's kiss.

The king forbade anyone in his kingdom to use a spinning wheel or even to keep a spindle in the house. But of course, this was to no avail. When the princess was almost 16, she wandered into a room where an old woman sat spinning. The woman had never heard the king's proclamation. Curious, the princess touched the spindle. She pricked her finger and fell to the floor in a deep sleep.

Almost immediately the good fairy arrived. Knowing that she would be lonely without those she loved, the fairy waved her magic wand and every living creature in the kingdom fell asleep too. (In some versions the king and queen were put to sleep, and in some they were not.) Then the fairy caused trees and brambles to spring up all around the castle and thorns to cover the walls, keeping the castle out of view except for the tops of the towers—and even these could only be seen from a great distance.

One hundred years later a king's son saw the towers of the castle, and an old peasant told him the story he had heard about the sleeping princess. Determined to find her, the prince entered the forest. As he walked, the briars and trees drew back to clear a path just for him. He passed sleeping lords, ladies, attendants, and pets as he went from room to room.

At last the prince came upon the beautiful sleeping princess. He leaned forward and kissed her. When he did, she—and then everyone else—awakened. The prince and princess fell in love and were married. The seven good fairies were invited to the marriage feast. The wicked old fairy was no longer a problem, for she died the moment the princess awakened.

# Questions & Activities Based Upon Bloom's Taxonomy

*Sleeping Beauty*

**Knowledge:**
1. What was the curse of the bad fairy?
2. Who are the members of Sleeping Beauty's family?
3. Name some of the gifts given by the good fairies.

**Comprehension:**
1. Tell why the people and animals in the castle went to sleep.
2. Explain how the curse of the bad fairy was changed.
3. Why did the old woman still have a spinning wheel?

**Application:**
1. Think of something you did when you weren't invited to a party.
2. What would you have given the princess as a gift if you were a fairy who was not invited to the party?
3. If you were Sleeping Beauty and received a gift you did not like, what would you do?

**Analysis:**
1. What are some daily activities in the life of a princess?
2. Compare and contrast Sleeping Beauty and Cinderella. How are they alike and how are they different?
3. How is Sleeping Beauty's life different from yours?

**Synthesis:**
1. How would the story have been different had the king and queen not angered the bad fairy?
2. Create a new ending for the story. Suppose Sleeping Beauty did not like the prince.
3. Plan a Welcome Back Ball for Sleeping Beauty. Discuss your plans with the class.

**Evaluation:**
1. List five things you would do if you were a prince or princess. Put them in order of importance.
2. Discuss the bad fairy's behavior. Was it right for her to act as she did? Why or why not?
3. Who is your favorite character in this story? Why?

## Design an invitation to a banquet being given in honor of the baby princess.

**Write a recipe for a cake to be served at Sleeping Beauty's party.**

## Decorate the cake.

Create a shoe box diorama of the castle with its walls of thorns.

Write a letter to the king. In it explain why you cannot attend the princess's party.

## Dear King,

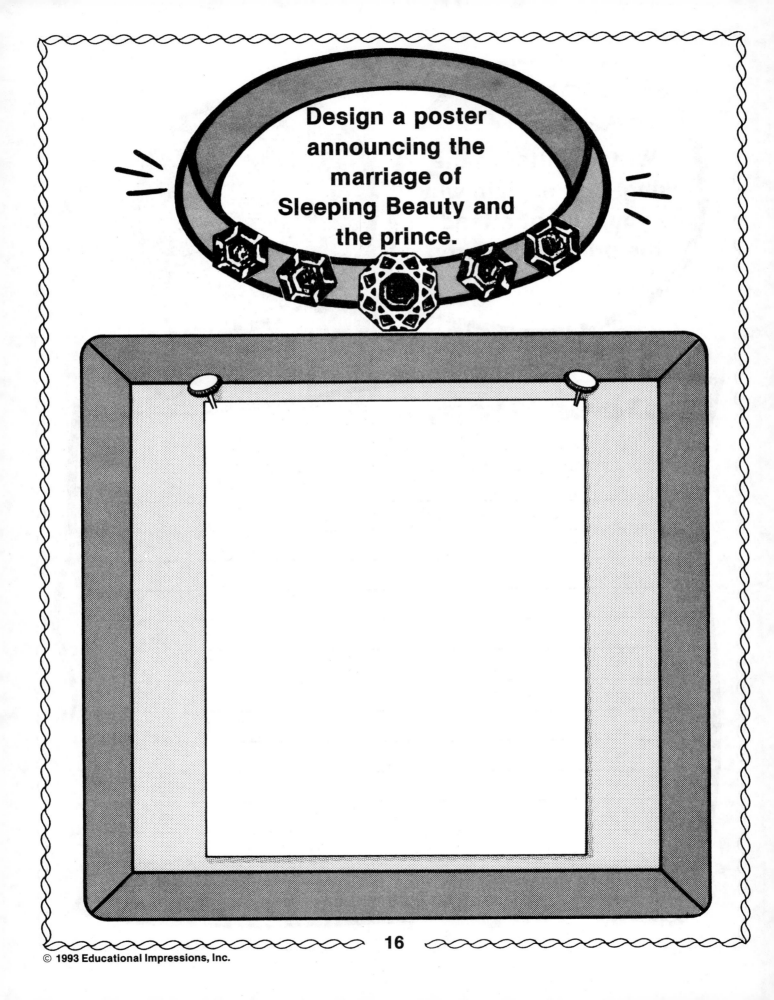

**Design a poster announcing the marriage of Sleeping Beauty and the prince.**

# Red Riding Hood

# Red Riding Hood

by the Brothers Grimm

## STORY SUMMARY

Once upon a time there lived a sweet little girl. Everyone loved her—especially her grandmother. In fact, the little girl got her nickname, Red Riding Hood, because she always wore the red velvet cloak that her grandmother had made for her.

One day Red Riding Hood's mother asked her to take some cake and wine to her grandmother, who was ill. She warned her not to loiter, but to go straight to grandmother's.

Along the way, Red Riding Hood met a wolf. Not knowing how wicked he was, she was not afraid. He began to question her, and she told him that she was bringing the basket to her grandmother. The wolf decided to get there first and to eat them both. He suggested to Red Riding Hood that she take her time and enjoy all that was around her. Forgetting her mother's warning to go straight to her grandmother's cottage, Red Riding Hood began to pick flowers.

When Red Riding Hood finally arrived at her grandmother's cottage, she was surprised to find the door open. She was even more surprised when she looked in the bed and saw how strange her grandmother looked. (Actually, it was the wolf in disguise. He had eaten the grandmother!)

"Oh, grandmother, what big eyes you have," said Red Riding Hood.

"The better to see you with," was the reply.

"Grandmother, what big ears you have," the little girl remarked.

"The better to hear you with, my dear," answered the wolf.

And so it went until, finally, Red Riding Hood noted, "But grandmother, what big teeth you have." This time the wolf, ready to show himself for what he really was, replied, "The better to eat you with, my dear," and he gobbled up Red Riding Hood, too!

When he finished his meal, the wolf went back to bed and before long he was snoring loudly. Luckily, a huntsman who was passing by heard the loud snoring and went in to see if the grandmother was all right. When he saw the wolf, he realized that he must have eaten the grandmother!

The huntsman cut open the wolf and saved both Red Riding Hood and her grandmother. Then he and Red Riding Hood filled the wolf with stones. When the wolf tried to escape, the stones dragged him back down and he fell down dead.

Everyone else was quite happy. The huntsman skinned the wolf and took the skin with him. The grandmother ate the cake and drank the wine and became strong again. And Red Riding Hood learned never to wander off against her mother's wishes!

Note: *Red Riding Hood* was first created by Charles Perrault. The endings of the two versions are quite different. You might want to read both to the children.

# Questions & Activities Based Upon Bloom's Taxonomy

*Red Riding Hood*

**Knowledge:**
1. What did Red Riding Hood's grandmother make for her?
2. Where did Red Riding Hood take the cake and wine?
3. How was the wolf disguised?

**Comprehension:**
1. Why did the wolf stop Red Riding Hood in the forest?
2. Tell how the wolf tricked Red Riding Hood as he talked to her in the forest.
3. Did the wolf's plan work? Explain.

**Application:**
1. What would you do if a stranger began to question you?
2. Have you ever felt frightened about something and couldn't explain why? Tell about your experience.
3. What advice can you give Red Riding Hood about strangers?

**Analysis:**
1. Read the story *The Three Little Pigs.* Compare the wolf in that story to the one in *Red Riding Hood.* How are they alike and how are they different?
2. List Red Riding Hood's good and bad qualities.
3. Tell about another version of *Red Riding Hood.* How are the two versions alike and different?

**Synthesis:**
1. Make up another way the wolf might have tricked Red Riding Hood into believing he was her grandmother.
2. Suppose Red Riding Hood knew as soon as she opened the door that the wolf had tricked her. How might the story have been different?
3. Create another character who might influence Red Riding Hood to do as her mother had told her.

**Evaluation:**
1. What lesson can be learned from this story?
2. Describe two good and two bad actions that happened in this story? Explain why you chose these actions.
3. How might Red Riding Hood persuade the hungry wolf not to eat her or her grandmother?

Design a
bumper sticker that
cautions children
about strangers.

## Draw your bumper sticker here.

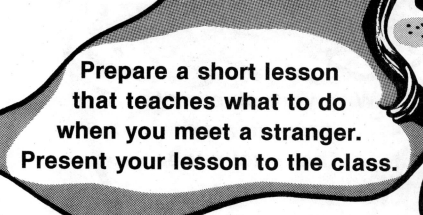

Prepare a short lesson
that teaches what to do
when you meet a stranger.
Present your lesson to the class.

## Stranger
## Danger

| Do's | Don'ts |
|------|--------|
|  |  |
|  |  |
|  |  |
|  |  |
|  |  |
|  |  |
|  |  |
|  |  |
|  |  |
|  |  |
|  |  |
|  |  |

**With your classmates prepare a skit that retells the story of Red Riding Hood.**

## Materials you will need:
### Red Hooded Cape
### Basket
### Wolf Mask
### Huntsman's Hat

Grandmother and Red Riding Hood have escaped from the wolf. Plan a party to celebrate.

**Use the plan sheet on the next page.**

# PLAN SHEET

PROJECT _____

SUPPLIES NEEDED_____

_____

_____

_____

_____

STEPS TO COMPLETE PROJECT _____

_____

_____

_____

_____

_____

_____

WHAT PROBLEMS DID YOU HAVE?_____

_____

_____

_____

HOW COULD YOU HAVE MADE THE PROJECT BETTER? _____

_____

_____

_____

# Write

**a newspaper article describing the wolf's attack on Red Riding Hood and her grandmother.**

_____

_____

_____

_____

_____

_____

_____

_____

_____

_____

_____

_____

_____

_____

_____

_____

# The Princess and the Pea

# The Princess and the Pea
## (or The Real Princess)

by Hans Christian Andersen

### STORY SUMMARY

There once was a prince who wanted to marry a princess, but he wanted to be certain that she was a *real* princess. He met many princesses, but there was something that was not quite right with each.

One day, during a dreadful storm, a young girl knocked at the palace door and asked for refuge. The girl was drenched; water streamed from her hair and from her clothes. She told the king and queen that she was a real princess. The queen decided to find out for sure.

Upon the bedstead, the queen placed three peas. Over the peas she lay twenty mattresses and twenty feather beds. Only a true princess, thought the queen, would be able to detect the peas.

The next morning the queen asked the girl how she had slept. Sure enough, the girl complained that something very hard under her had kept her from having a restful sleep. The prince was convinced that the girl was indeed a true princess, and the two were married.

This, we are told, is a true story.

# Questions & Activities Based Upon Bloom's Taxonomy

*The Princess and the Pea*

**Knowledge:**
1. Why was the prince sad?
2. Who opened the gate on that stormy night?
3. What streamed from the princess's hair?

**Comprehension:**
1. Why did the prince have a hard time choosing a bride?
2. Describe the test used on the princess.
3. What brought the princess to the castle doors?

**Application:**
1. What might be placed in your bed that could cause you a sleepless night?
2. How many pillows or mattresses would have to be placed over it before you could fall asleep?
3. What are three things you would like to know about the prince or princess if you were about to marry him or her?

**Analysis:**
1. What other fairy tale is similar to this one? Give a brief summary of it.
2. What type of character do you think the prince is? List some of his qualities.
3. Categorize this fairy tale on a scale of one to ten. One is if you think the story is not good. Ten is if you think it is great. Explain why you rated it as you did.

**Synthesis:**
1. Create at least three other tests to find a true princess. Describe them.
2. How would the story have been different had the princess not passed the test?
3. Suppose the prince had fallen in love with a poor girl. How might the story be different?

**Evaluation:**
1. Was it right for the queen to test the princess without the princess knowing about it? Why or why not?
2. Is it very important for the prince to marry a princess? Why or why not?
3. Is this really a true story? Explain your answer.

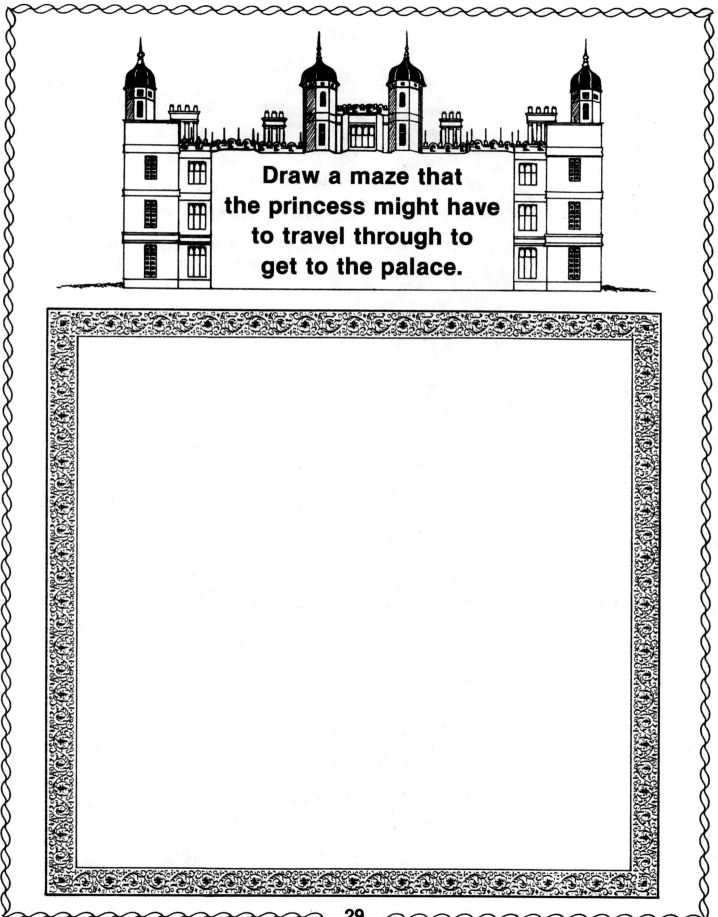

**Draw a maze that
the princess might have
to travel through to
get to the palace.**

Write a short wedding march for the royal wedding. Begin with, "Here comes the princess. . ."

**Write a short skit of the prince and princess's wedding. Ask a few of your classmates to act in your skit.**

## Draw a picture of the wedding here.

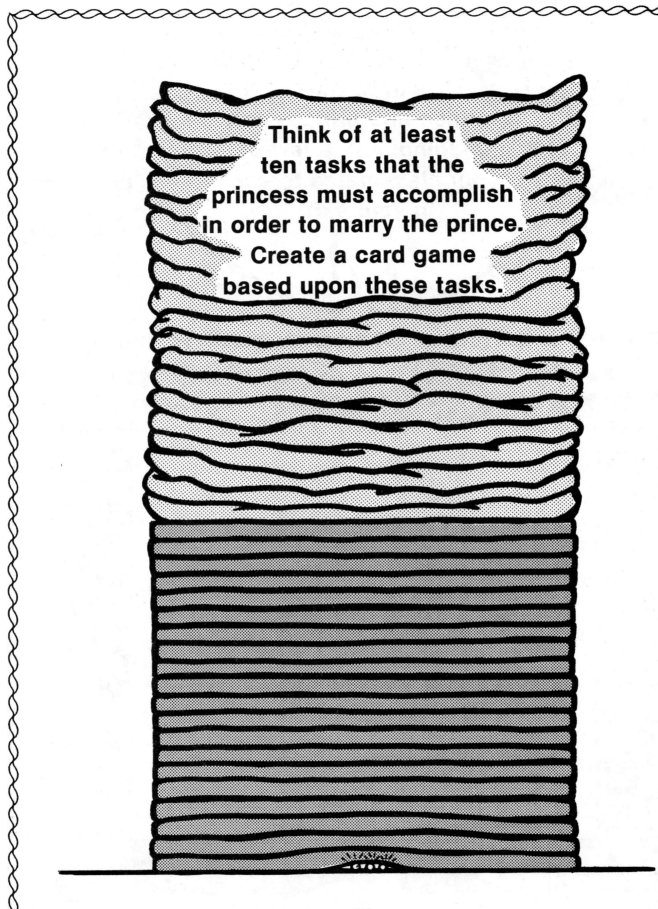

**Think of at least ten tasks that the princess must accomplish in order to marry the prince. Create a card game based upon these tasks.**

Design a wedding gown for the princess.

## Draw a picture of the gown here.

# Jack and the Beanstalk

# Jack and the Beanstalk

## STORY SUMMARY

Once upon a time there was a boy named Jack. His mother sent him to the market to sell their cow so that they would have money on which to live. But instead of getting money for the cow, Jack sold it for a handful of magical beans. When his mother learned what Jack had done, she sent him to bed without his supper and threw the beans out of the window.

When Jack awoke the next morning, he saw that a huge beanstalk had grown past his attic window and up to the sky. Jack jumped out of his window and onto the beanstalk. Higher and higher he climbed until he reached the sky. There he found a road that led to a very tall house. On the doorstep of the house stood a woman.

Jack begged the woman for some breakfast. Warning him that her husband was a giant ogre who ate little boys, she finally agreed to let Jack into the house. Before Jack could finish his bread, cheese and milk, however, Jack and the woman heard the ogre coming. Quickly, Jack hid in the oven.

The ogre was sure that he smelled someone there and said to his wife, "Fee-fi-fo-fum, I smell the blood of an Englishman. Be he alive, or be he dead, I'll have his bones to grind my bread." But his wife convinced him that it was just the scraps of yesterday's dinner that he smelled.

Finally, the ogre left the room and Jack was able to escape. When he did, he took one of the ogre's bags of gold.

Jack and his mother lived on the gold for quite a while. When the gold ran out, Jack again climbed the beanstalk and went to the ogre's home. Again he convinced the ogre's wife to let him in. Again the ogre was made to believe that he didn't really smell the blood of an Englishman. And again Jack escaped—this time with the ogre's hen that lay golden eggs.

One day Jack, who had gotten quite greedy, decided to pay another visit to the ogre's home. Knowing that the wife would no longer trust him, this time he hid from both the ogre and his wife. He waited until the ogre fell asleep and then ran away with the ogre's harp. But the harp cried out and woke the giant.

The ogre chased Jack, but Jack managed to climb down the beanstalk before the giant jumped onto it. Jack called to his mother to bring him an axe. With two chops, he cut down the beanstalk and put an end to the ogre. Jack and his mother became very rich. Jack married a princess and lived happily ever after.

# Questions & Activities Based Upon Bloom's Taxonomy

## Jack and the Beanstalk

**Knowledge:**
1. List the three treasures that Jack stole from the giant.
2. What did the man Jack met on the way to town have?
3. What did Jack's mother do with the magic beans?

**Comprehension:**
1. Who is the main character of this story?
2. List the other characters and describe each.
3. Explain what is meant by the giant's famous refrain.

**Application:**
1. What is meant by magic? Give three examples of magic.
2. How might you have tricked the giant out of his treasures?
3. Describe a typical meal for the giant. Describe a typical meal for you.

**Analysis:**
1. Compare the treasures in this fairy tale to those in another. How are they alike and how are they different?
2. Make a mental diagram of the story events. Explain it to the class.
3. Categorize the characters into good and evil categories. Explain why you placed each as you did.

**Synthesis:**
1. How might the story have been different had Jack allowed the giant to climb down and reach the ground?
2. Develop a new way for Jack to get up and down the beanstalk quickly. Explain your invention to the class.
3. Predict how Jack's and his mother's lives will be different now that they are no longer poor.

**Evaluation:**
1. Did the giant's behavior make it okay for Jack to do what he did? Explain.
2. If you could change the giant and give him different qualities, what changes would you make? Why?
3. Give three reasons why you would or would not recommend the reading of this story to a friend.

The giant is tired of saying, "Fee-fi-fo-fum...." Make up a new set of words that the giant could use.

Create two more
treasures that the
giant might own.

## Draw a picture of the treasures.

Plan a giant hunt in which Jack leads his friends in a fight against the giant.

## Describe your plan here.

**Design another place for the giant to live where he won't be able to harm anyone. Paint a picture of this place.**

# Write a short paragraph about the giant's new home.

_____

_____

_____

_____

_____

_____

_____

**40**

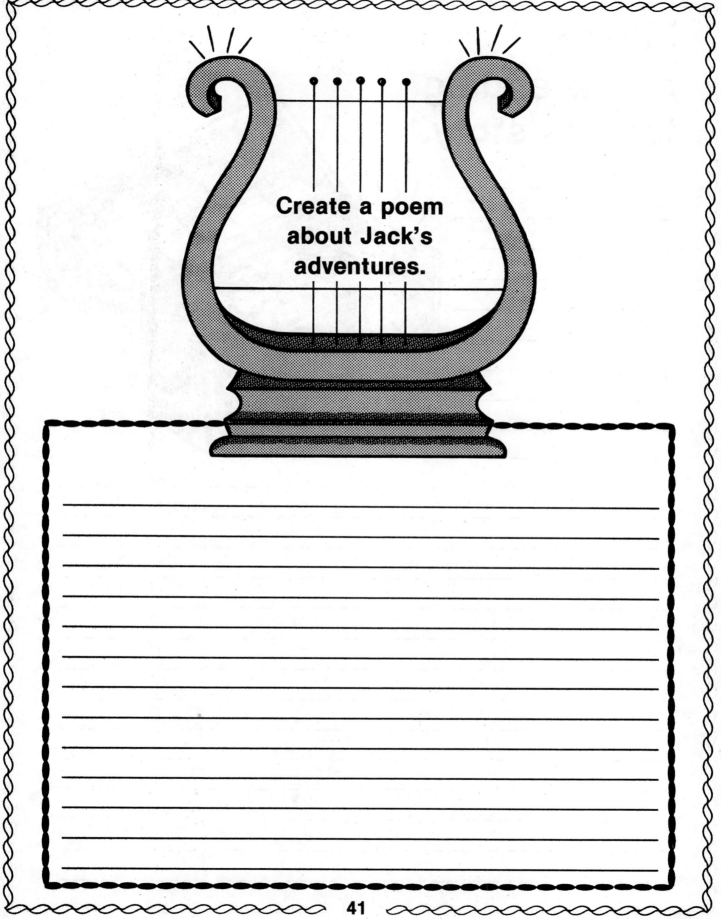

Create a poem
about Jack's
adventures.

# Write
## a new ending for this story.

# Rumpelstiltskin

# Rumpelstiltskin

by the Brothers Grimm

## STORY SUMMARY

Once upon a time there lived a poor miller with a beautiful daughter. The miller bragged to the king that his daughter could spin straw into gold. The king told the miller to bring the girl to the palace so that he could test her skill. He warned that if she failed, she would die.

The girl was taken to a room filled with straw and was given a spinning wheel and a reel. Of course, she had no idea how to spin straw into gold and she soon began to cry. Suddenly, a strange little man entered the room. He offered to do it for her in return for her necklace. By morning, all the straw was spun into gold.

When the king returned and found the gold, he ordered her to spin a larger amount by the next day. Again the girl began to cry, and again the little man appeared. This time he agreed to spin the straw into gold in return for her ring.

When the king found that the miller's daughter had succeeded at this task, too, he had her sent into an even larger straw-filled room. If she could spin all of the straw into gold, she would become his queen. Once more, the girl began to cry and once more the little man appeared. This time, however, the girl had nothing to give.

The little man said that he would spin the straw into gold if only she would promise to give him her first born child if she becomes queen. Not knowing what else to do, she agreed.

The miller's daughter did become queen and soon forgot her promise to the strange little man. A year later she had a beautiful child. It was then that the little man re-appeared to claim the child. Heartbroken, the queen tried to talk him into taking all her riches instead, but he refused. The little man did pity her, however, and agreed that if she could guess his name in three days, she could keep her child.

The queen sent out a messenger to find out all the strange and curious names there might be. On the first day and the second the queen guessed every name she could think of, but to each the little man replied, "That is not my name." On the third day, however, the messenger came with interesting news. He had seen a ridiculous little man hopping around a fire and shouting:

"Today I bake, tomorrow I brew,
The next I'll have the young queen's child;
How glad I am that no one knew,
That Rumpelstiltskin I am styled."

When the little man came later that day, the queen made two wrong guesses. But on the third try she said to his surprise, "Perhaps Rumpelstiltskin is your name."

In a rage, Rumpelstiltskin plunged into the Earth. He pulled at his leg so hard that he tore himself in two.

# Questions & Activities Based Upon Bloom's Taxonomy

*Rumpelstiltskin*

**Knowledge:**
1. What did the miller say his daughter could do?
2. Name the things the miller's daughter gave the man.
3. How long did it take to spin the straw into gold?

**Comprehension:**
1. Why did the girl promise to give the little man her first born child should she become queen?
2. What would have happened to the miller's daughter if the straw hadn't been turned to gold?
3. What problems did the miller's bragging cause?

**Application:**
1. If you were a miller, what work would you perform?
2. If you were the miller's daughter, what would you have done when told to spin the straw into gold?
3. If you were the queen, what names would you guess?

**Analysis:**
1. Discuss the queen's good and bad qualities.
2. Categorize the characters into good and bad. Discuss your reasons.
3. Compare Rumpelstiltskin to the wicked fairy in Sleeping Beauty. How are they alike and how are they different?

**Synthesis:**
1. Create another way for the miller's daughter to become queen.
2. Design another task the miller's daughter might perform besides spinning straw into gold.
3. What might have happened had the queen not found out the little man's name? How might she have prevented this?

**Evaluation:**
1. Was it right for the miller to brag to the king?
2. What kind of parent do you think Rumpelstiltskin would have been? Give reasons for your answer.
3. Pretend you are the queen. How would feel about your father?

Create a puppet of Rumpelstiltskin. Design it so that it can break in half as he did at the end of the story.

**Create a new rhyme that Rumpelstiltskin might sing about his name.**

_____
_____
_____
_____
_____
_____
_____
_____
_____
_____
_____
_____

**Make a jigsaw puzzle of one of the characters in the story.**

# How to Make Your Jigsaw Puzzle:

Draw a picture of your character.

Color the picture.

Glue it onto tag board.

Cut the picture into pieces.

## Challenge your friends to solve your puzzle.

**Choose a character from the story and do a character profile.**

_____

_____

_____

_____

_____

_____

_____

_____

_____

_____

_____

Use the chart on the next page for ideas.

# CHARACTER PROFILE

**Name:** _____

**Height:** _____

**Weight:** _____

**Coloring:** _____

       **Eyes:** _____

       **Hair:** _____

       **Skin:** _____

**Personality:** _____

_____

_____

_____

_____

_____

**Hobbies:** _____

_____

_____

_____

_____

_____

_____

**50**

# Cinderella

## by Charles Perrault

## STORY SUMMARY

Forced by her cruel stepmother and stepsisters to do all the work, Cinderella often sat by the chimney when her work was done. In fact, this is how she got her name; they called her Cinderella because she was always covered with cinders.

One day the king's son gave a ball to which Cinderella's stepsisters were invited. Cinderella helped them dress and fix their hair, and when they left for the ball, she began to cry, for she, too, wanted to go.

Suddenly, Cinderella's fairy godmother appeared and told her that she would see to it that she could go. The fairy godmother turned a pumpkin into a beautiful coach; six mice into six horses; a rat into a coachman; and six lizards into footmen. Then she turned Cinderella's rags into a beautiful gown and gave her a lovely pair of little glass slippers. As the coach pulled away, the fairy godmother warned Cinderella to leave before the stroke of midnight. She told her that at midnight all would be as it was before the magic spell.

Cinderella arrived at the ball, and the prince fell in love with her at first sight. The two danced all night. Then, at 11:45, Cinderella ran off as quickly as she could. She arrived home just before her stepsisters. When her stepsisters returned, they told Cinderella about the beautiful princess who had appeared at the ball.

The next night the ball was to continue. Again, as soon as the stepsisters left, Cinderella's fairy godmother appeared, and Cinderella, too, went to the ball. This time, however, Cinderella almost forgot to leave. When she heard the first stroke of midnight, she fled. But as she did, she dropped one of her glass slippers.

The prince found the slipper and pronounced that he would marry the maiden whose foot fit the slipper. His servant carried the slipper from home to home and tried it on all the young maidens. At last he came to the home of Cinderella and her stepsisters. Each stepsister tried to squeeze her foot into the slipper, but could not. When Cinderella asked to try it on, her stepsisters laughed. But the gentleman said that he had been ordered to try it on *all* the young ladies of the kingdom.

Of course, the slipper fit perfectly. What's more, Cinderella had the mate in her pocket. Cinderella and the prince were married. Being kind as well as beautiful, Cinderella forgave her stepsisters. She gave them a home in the palace and married them to two lords of the court.

Note: The Brothers Grimm also wrote a version of *Cinderella.* The endings of the two versions are quite different. You might want to read both to the children. You might also want to read the Disney version to them.

# Questions & Activities Based Upon Bloom's Taxonomy

*Cinderella*

**Knowledge:**
1. How many people were in Cinderella's family?
2. Who made it possible for Cinderella to go to the ball?
3. What did Cinderella lose on the palace steps?

**Comprehension:**
1. Explain why Cinderella couldn't complain to her father.
2. How did Cinderella help her stepsisters prepare for the ball?
3. Explain how Cinderella's fairy godmother helped her.

**Application:**
1. If you were Cinderella's friend, how might you have helped her?
2. Pretend that you are Cinderella. How did you feel when you saw yourself in the mirror after your fairy godmother finished with you.
3. If you were Cinderella, how would you treat your stepsisters now that you are a princess?

**Analysis:**
1. List some of the stepmother's good and bad qualities.
2. Choose one character from the story and write a character sketch.
3. If you were Cinderella, how might you try to change your stepmother's feelings toward you?

**Synthesis:**
1. If Cinderella's stepmother had showed love for her, how might the story have been different?
2. What might have happened to Cinderella had she not married the prince?
3. Create a new name for Cinderella now that she is a princess. Explain why you chose that name.

**Evaluation:**
1. Why, do you think, did the stepmother treat Cinderella as she did?
2. Which would you choose: to live with your family in your home or to live in a palace as a prince or princess?
3. Did you like this story? Why or why not?

**Create a ball gown for Cinderella.**

## Draw Cinderella in her gown.

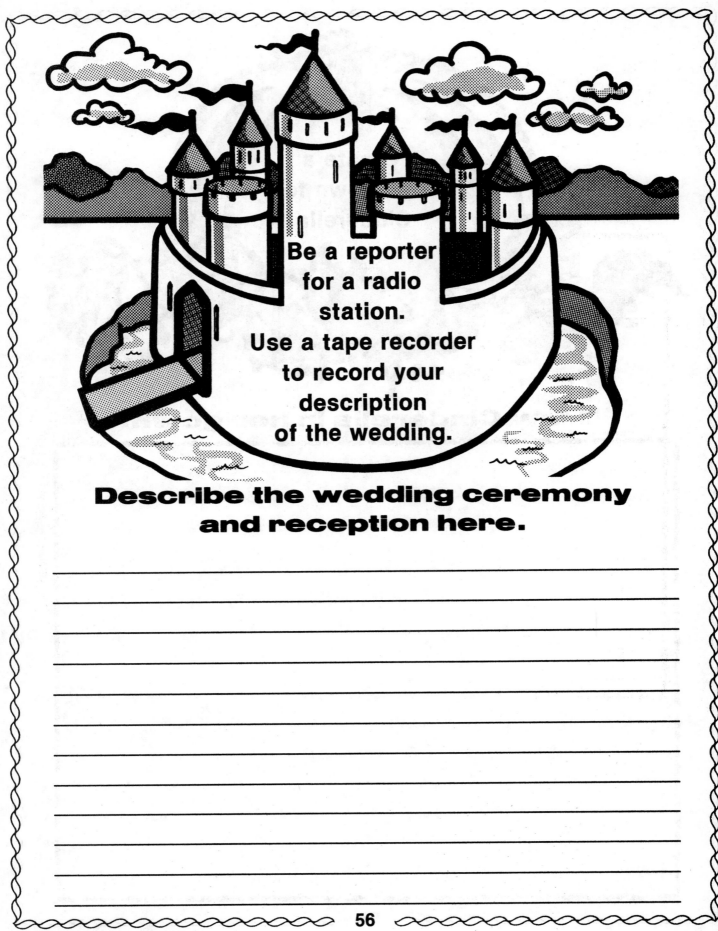

Be a reporter
for a radio
station.
Use a tape recorder
to record your
description
of the wedding.

## Describe the wedding ceremony and reception here.

_____

_____

_____

_____

_____

_____

_____

_____

_____

_____

_____

As Cinderella, write a thank you note to your fairy godmother for all that she has done.

**Dear Fairy Godmother,**

_____

_____

_____

_____

_____

_____

_____

_____

_____

_____

_____

_____

Draw a comic strip that shows Cinderella's stepsisters trying to make the slipper fit.

# Write
## about Cinderella's life after she marries the prince.

_____

_____

_____

_____

_____

_____

_____

_____

_____

_____

_____

_____

_____

_____

_____

_____

_____

# Jorinda and Joringel

# Jorinda and Joringel

## by the Brothers Grimm

### STORY SUMMARY

There lived a witch who in the daytime took the shape of a cat or a screech owl and at night the shape of a human. Anyone who came within one hundred paces of her castle was put under a spell and not allowed to stir until she decided to free him. If an innocent maiden came, she changed her into a bird and shut her up in a cage.

One day the beautiful Jorinda and the handsome Joringel walked together in the forest. The two were betrothed and very much in love and they wanted to talk quietly. Unfortunately, the two young lovers strayed too close to the witch's castle. Appearing as a screech owl, the witch turned Jorinda into a nightingale and forced Joringel to stand like a stone, unable to speak.

After a while the witch allowed Joringel to leave, but she would not heed his pleas to give him back his Jorinda. Joringel went away and for a long time tended sheep in a strange village.

One night Joringel dreamed that he found a blood-red flower with a beautiful pearl in the center. In his dream he used the flower to free from enchantment everything he touched. When he awoke, Joringel set out to find such a flower.

On the ninth day, Joringel found a blood-red flower with a dewdrop as large as a pearl. He took it and set out for the witch's castle. To his relief, he was not held fast when he came within one hundred paces of it.

Joringel touched the castle door with the flower, and the door flew open. When the witch saw him, she bacame very angry, but Joringel just ignored her. He searched among the cages and tried to figure out which nightingale was his beloved Jorinda.

As he searched, he noticed that the witch was trying to escape with one of the cages. Joringel sprang towards her and with the flower touched both her and the cage she was holding. The witch would never again have the ability to harm anyone with her spells.

Almost immediately, Jorinda appeared before him, as beautiful as ever. Joringel then touched all the other birds and changed them, too, back to their proper form.

A short time later Jorinda and Joringel were married. The two lived happily ever after.

# Questions & Activities Based Upon Bloom's Taxonomy

*Jorinda and Joringel*

**Knowledge:**
1. How did the witch appear in the daytime?
2. What did the maidens who neared the witch's castle become?
3. What form did the witch take during the night?

**Comprehension:**
1. Explain why Jorinda and Joringel were walking in the forest.
2. Describe what happened to Joringel and Jorinda when they strayed near the castle.
3. Describe Joringel's dream.

**Application:**
1. Retell this story in your own words.
2. What would you have done if you had been in Joringel's place?
3. Why did Joringel dream of the flower?

**Analysis:**
1. Compare the witch in this story with the fairy godmother in Cinderella. Describe their likes and differences.
2. How would you react if the witch cast a spell on your parents? What would you do?
3. What are some other fairy tales written by the Grimm Brothers? What do these tales have in common?

**Synthesis:**
1. Describe how Jorinda's life as a bird might have been.
2. Create a story about the witch after she loses her magical powers.
3. Plan another way of escape for Jorinda.

**Evaluation:**
1. If you lived in a town near the castle of the wicked witch, what could you do to prevent the witch from casting her spell on unaware travelers?
2. Why, do you think, did the witch cast such an evil spell on the maidens?
3. Where do you think Jorinda and Joringel will live? Why?

Act out the scene in the story where Jorinda and Joringel fall prey to the witch's spell.

SCENE 1
TAKE 2

Draw a picture of Jorinda as a bird.

Stage
a debate
between the witch
and Joringel. The
witch will try
to persuade her
judges (classmates)
that her actions
were justified.
Joringel will try to prove
that they were not.

Plan a great party to welcome back all of the maidens.

## Describe your decorations here.

## Write out a menu for the evening meal.

# MENU

# Write

## a narrative paragraph describing Jorinda's life as a bird.

_____

_____

_____

_____

_____

_____

_____

_____

_____

_____

_____

_____

_____

_____

_____

_____

_____

_____

# Hansel and Gretel

# Hansel and Gretel

## by the Brothers Grimm

### STORY SUMMARY

Near a great forest lived a poor woodcutter, his wife and his two children. The boy was named Hansel and the girl, Gretel. There was a great famine and the poor woodcutter didn't know how he would feed his children when there was scarcely enough for him and his wife.

The man's wife convinced him to take the children out into the forest and abandon them with only a piece of bread for each. The next day their father and stepmother led them deep into the forest. But the children had overheard their conversation, and as they walked, Hansel left a trail of white pebbles. When they reached the middle of the forest, their father and stepmother went off to chop some wood and said that they would return shortly.

The children fell asleep and when they awoke, they were still alone. Gretel began to cry, but Hansel comforted her and said that they would find their home by the light of the full moon. Hansel then took his little sister by the hand and followed the shiny pebbles back to their father's home. Their father, sorry for what he had done, rejoiced at seeing them.

However, a short time later another famine hit the land, and the stepmother again insisted that they abandon the children—this time deeper into the forest. The father was heart-broken, but because he had agreed to the plan the first time, he had to agree again. ("Anyone who says A must also say B.")

This time Hansel was unable to gather pebbles, for the stepmother had locked the door. Instead, Hansel dropped crumbs of bread along the trail. But when he looked for the crumbs, he found that the birds had eaten them and there was nothing for them to follow.

Deeper and deeper into the woods they went, until finally they came upon a house made of bread, cakes and candy. Hansel began to eat the roof and Gretel, the window. As they nibbled, a very old woman appeared. She pretended to be kind, but she was really a wicked witch who ate little children.

The next morning, the witch seized Hansel and put him into a cage. She intended to fatten him up until he was fat enough to eat. Each morning the witch asked Hansel to stick out his finger, but each time the clever Hansel stuck out a bone instead. The witch was easily fooled, for her eyesight was very poor.

Finally, the witch got tired of waiting. She told Gretel that they would bake the bread and ordered her to go into the oven to test it. Gretel knew that the witch planned to shove her in the oven and to eat her, too. She asked the witch to show her how to do it, and when the witch put her head in the oven, Gretel pushed her all the way in and locked the door.

With the witch dead, Gretel was able to free Hansel. The children gathered the witch's jewels and put them in their pockets. Then they walked and walked until they came to a body of water with no bridge. Luckily, a kind duck took each across on its back.

At last Hansel and Gretel found their way home. Their father, now a widow, had not had a happy moment since abandoning his children and was delighted to see them. The three of them, now rich because of the witch's jewels, lived happily ever after.

# Questions & Activities Based Upon Bloom's Taxonomy

*Hansel and Gretel*

**Knowledge:**
1. Who are the main characters in this story?
2. Where did the father and stepmother lead the children?
3. What did Hansel and Gretel find in the forest?

**Comprehension:**
1. Why did the stepmother want to get rid of the children?
2. How did Hansel plan to find his way home?
3. How did Hansel fool the witch?

**Application:**
1. The family in this story did not have enough food to eat. If your family had a similar problem, how might you help?
2. If you had been Gretel, how might you have delayed the witch from eating Hansel?
3. Describe the little house in the woods. Why, do you think, did the witch make it like this?

**Analysis:**
1. Compare the stepmother in this story with the stepmother in Cinderella. How are they alike? How are they different?
2. Suppose the father had burst in on the witch as she was about to eat Hansel. What might he have done?
3. Why, do you think, are the stepmothers in fairy tales usually cruel? Explain the reasoning behind your answer.

**Synthesis:**
1. Hansel used a chicken bone to trick the witch. Create another way he could have tricked her.
2. This story had a happy ending. Create a different ending where the children do not find their way home. How will their lives be different?
3. Plan a good way for Hansel and Gretel to use their money.

**Evaluation:**
1. Which character would you like to be and why?
2. What valuable lesson can be learned from this story?
3. Judge the father's decision to go along with his wife's plan to abandon the children.

70

Design your own candy house.
If you cannot make a real one,
draw and color one
according to your plans.

## Use the plan sheet on the next page.

# PLAN SHEET

PROJECT _____

SUPPLIES NEEDED_____

_____

_____

_____

_____

**STEPS TO COMPLETE PROJECT** _____

_____

_____

_____

_____

_____

_____

**WHAT PROBLEMS DID YOU HAVE?**_____

_____

_____

_____

_____

**HOW COULD YOU HAVE MADE THE PROJECT BETTER?** _____

_____

_____

_____

_____

Write a letter to the stepmother. Tell her how wrong it was to lose Hansel and Gretel in the forest.

## Dear Stepmother,

Draw
a map
to the
witch's
house.

**Plan and teach a lesson to your classmates about staying away from strangers.**

## Ideas:

_____
_____
_____
_____
_____
_____
_____
_____
_____
_____
_____
_____
_____
_____
_____

# The Little Match Girl

# The Little Match Girl

## by Hans Christian Andersen

### STORY SUMMARY

It was a cold and snowy last day of the old year. A poor little girl wandered the streets trying to sell her matches, but she had not sold even one the entire day.

The little girl was very hungry and very cold. Her bare feet were almost frozen from the bitter cold. When she started out, she had been wearing her mother's slippers, buy they were much too large for her and had fallen off her feet along the way.

Finally, the little girl crouched down in a corner and drew her feet close under her. She took out a match and lit it. Then she held her hands around the flame to warm them. As she watched the flame, it seemed to her that she was sitting in front of a beautiful brass stove. But when the fire went out, all that was there were the remains of the burned-out match.

The little girl lit another match, and as the light fell upon the wall, she could see a table beautifully set. A glorious goose seemed to come right to her. But when the match went out, only a cold wall was before her.

The little girl lit the third match. This time a beautiful Christmas tree appeared. Just as she reached out to touch the ornaments, however, the match went out. Still, the lights on the tree burned brighter and brighter and rose into the sky, becoming the twinkling stars. One of the lights fell down and streaked across the sky. "Someone is dying," thought the little girl. Her grandmother, the only person ever to really love her, had told her before she died that when a star fell down, a soul rose up to heaven.

The little girl lit one more match. Right before her eyes appeared her grandmother! The little girl begged her grandmother to take her with her, for she feared that she, too, would disappear when the flame went out. Quickly, she lit a whole bunch of matches to try to keep her grandmother with her. The grandmother took the little girl in her arms, and they both soared above the earth to a place where neither cold nor hunger is known.

In the morning, the little match girl was found frozen to death. Strangely, however, her lips were smiling. The people who found her could not imagine the beautiful things she had seen. They had no idea that she and her grandmother had gone into the new year with such joy and gladness.

# Questions & Activities Based Upon Bloom's Taxonomy

## *The Little Match Girl*

**Knowledge:**
1. What was the little girl trying to sell?
2. How was the litte girl dressed?
3. On what day of the year did the story take place?

**Comprehension:**
1. Why did the girl crouch down near a corner of the building?
2. Why did the girl light a whole bunch of matches?
3. Why is New Year's Eve called such?

**Application:**
1. Write three questions you would like to ask the match girl about her life.
2. If the match girl were your friend, how might you help her?
3. Describe a meal you have on a holiday.

**Analysis:**
1. Compare your life to the life of the little match girl. How are they alike and how are they different?
2. How would you feel if you were made to go out into the cold with no warm clothing?
3. Make a list of the characters in this story. Now categorize the list.

**Synthesis:**
1. Create a new, happier ending for the story.
2. Describe the match girl's new life after leaving with her grandmother.
3. Invent a way to help poor or abused children all over the world.

**Evaluation:**
1. How do you feel about this story? Why do you feel this way?
2. What valuable lesson can be learned from this story?
3. What would you have done if you had passed the match girl as she sat in the cold?

An elegy is a poem that expresses grief that someone has died. Write an elegy for the little match girl.

RIP

_____
_____
_____
_____
_____
_____
_____
_____
_____
_____
_____
_____
_____
_____

**Design a diorama
of a scene
from the story.**

## List the materials you will use.

_____

_____

_____

_____

_____

_____

_____

_____

_____

_____

_____

_____

Create a bulletin board display that shows compassion for the homeless and less fortunate people of the world.

**Sketch your ideas here.**

**Create a poem to cheer the match girl.**

**Write your poem here.**

_____

_____

_____

_____

_____

_____

_____

_____

_____

_____

# Write

a letter to the Little Match Girl's father. Tell him how you feel about the way she is being treated.

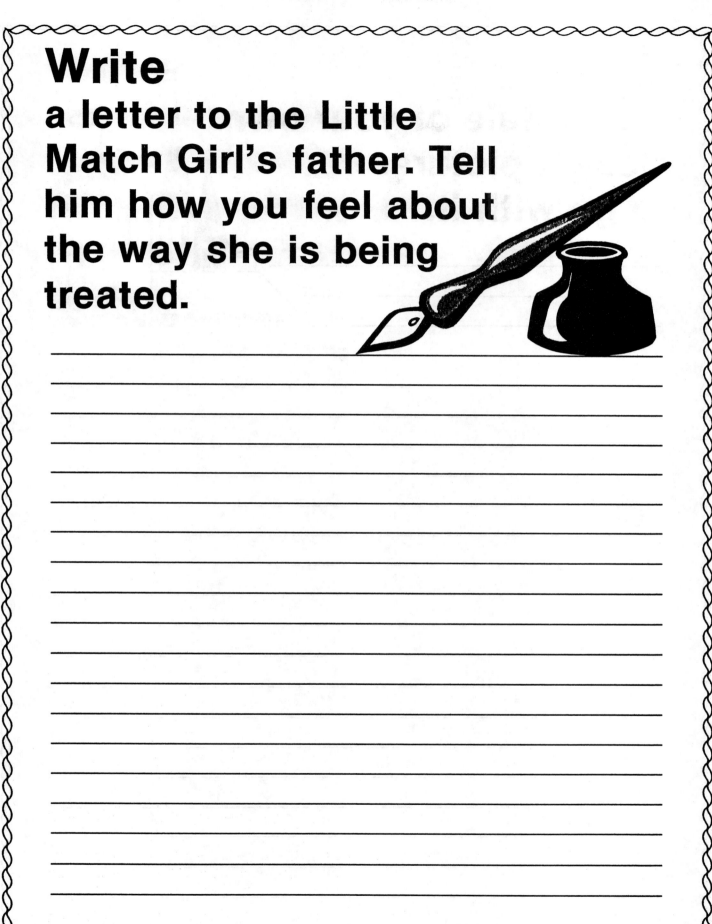

_____

_____

_____

_____

_____

_____

_____

_____

_____

_____

_____

_____

_____

_____

_____

_____

# Write
## a fairy tale of your own. Design pictures to go with it.

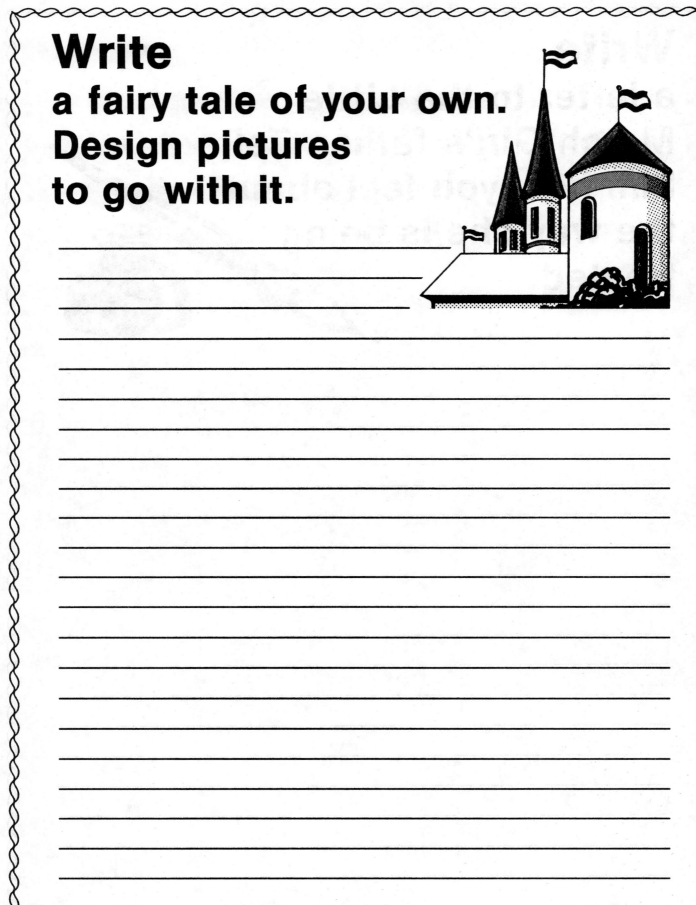

_____

_____

_____

_____

_____

_____

_____

_____

_____

_____

_____

_____

_____

_____

_____

_____

_____

_____

# Bookmarks

Color and decorate your bookmark. Use it when reading your favorite fairy tale or other storybook.

85

# Hansel & Gretel
# Finger Puppets

Use these patterns to make finger puppets. You will need a piece of cardboard for each puppet. Color your puppets. Add or change any details you wish.

Use the puppets to put on a skit about Hansel and Gretel.

# Scrambled Fairy Tale Characters

Can you unscramble the letters to figure out these fairy tale characters?

1. I C N E D R E L A L _ _ _ _ _ _ _ _ _ _

2. D E R  G N I D I R  D O O H _ _ _  _ _ _ _ _ _  _ _ _ _

3. S E L H A N _ _ _ _ _ _

4. W S N O  H W I T E _ _ _ _  _ _ _ _ _

5. L W O F _ _ _ _

6. P S L E E I N G  T Y B E A U _ _ _ _ _ _ _ _ _  _ _ _ _ _ _

7. O J R N I E G L _ _ _ _ _ _ _ _

8. C I W T H _ _ _ _ _

87

# Fairy Tale Magic Game

## DIRECTIONS

1. Copy or remove the gameboard sheets on pages 89 through 92. Mount them on heavy board.

2. Copy or remove page 103, which has pictures of the characters. Cut out the pictures and the stands and mount them on heavy board.

3. Copy or remove pages 93-102 and cut out the Question and Chance Cards.

4. Have each player choose a character. Two to six players (or teams of players) can play.

5. In clockwise fashion, each player draws a question card. If the player answers the question correctly, he/she moves ahead the number of spaces indicated on the card.

6. If the player lands on Chance, he/she draws a chance card. The player will move forward or backward as indicated on the card.

7. The first player to get back around to Start wins the game.


Note: The Fairy Tale Magic Game pages have been perforated for ease in removal; however, you may prefer to make copies of these pages and to keep the pages in the book for future reference.

Fairy
Ma

Question
Cards

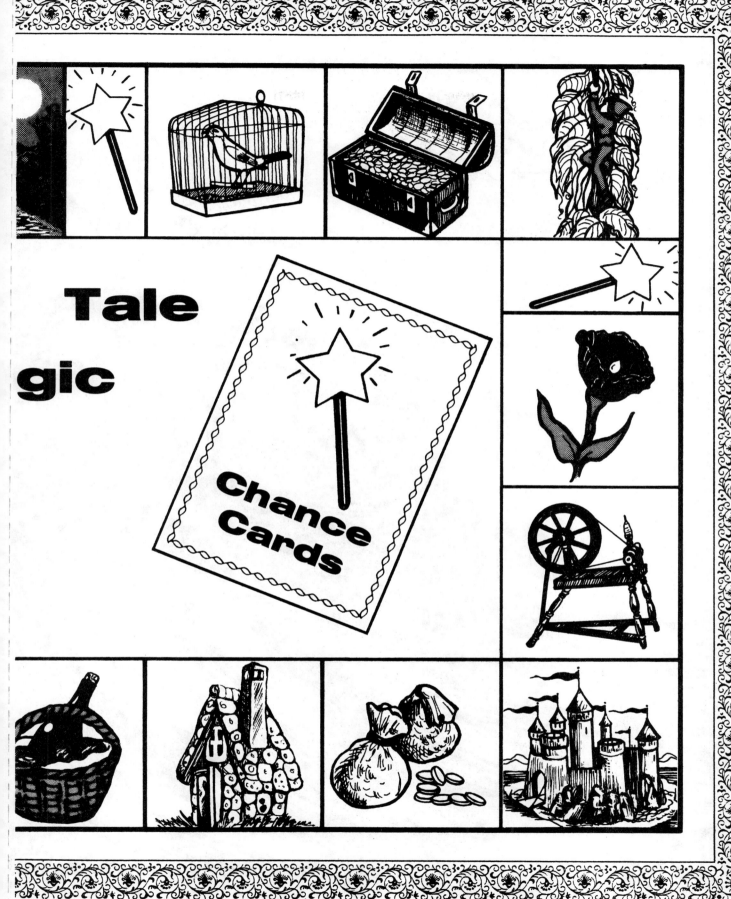

Tale
gic

Chance
Cards

Where did Cinderella
go to meet the prince?

(Move 1 space.)

Why did the little match
girl light the first
match?

(Move 2 spaces.)

What was the witch's
house made from in the
story *Hansel and Gretel*.

(Move 2 spaces.)

Explain what
happened to
Rumpelstiltskin
when the queen
guessed his name.

(Move 2 spaces.)

How did Cinderella
lose her slipper?

(Move 3 spaces.)

How did Joringel
find Jorinda?

(Move 1 space.)

What caused Jorinda to
turn into a bird?

(Move 2 spaces.)

How did the queen find
out that the strange
little man was named
Rumpelstiltskin?

(Move 2 spaces.)

**Question**

**Question**

**Question**

**Question**

**Question**

**Question**

**Question**

**Question**

94

Into what did the princess in *Rumpelstitlskin* have to spin straw?

(Move 2 spaces.)

What did Gretel do to the wicked witch?

(Move 3 spaces.)

How many years did Sleeping Beauty sleep?

(Move 2 spaces.)

What is a famous quote from *Snow White and the Seven Dwarfs*?

(Move 3 spaces.)

Why was Snow White's stepmother jealous of her?

(Move 2 spaces.)

How did the wicked queen trick Snow White into opening the door?

(Move 2 spaces.)

Who is the main character in *The Sleeping Beauty?*

(Move 2 spaces.)

Where did Cinderella go after she left the ball?

(Move 1 space.)

**Question**

**Question**

**Question**

**Question**

**Question**

**Question**

**Question**

**Question**

96

What is the setting
for *Hansel and Gretel?*

(Move 3 spaces.)

How did the young fairy
change the wicked old
fairy's spell upon
Sleeping Beauty?

(Move 2 spaces.)

What is the main idea of
the story *Jack and the
Beanstalk?*

(Move 2 spaces.)

Why couldn't the
princess in *The
Princess and the Pea*
get a good night's
sleep?

(Move 1 space.)

Whom did
little Red Riding Hood
meet in the woods?

(Move 2 spaces.)

Why was Red Riding
Hood taking cake to
her grandmother?

(Move 3 spaces.)

How did Red Riding
Hood get her name?

(Move 2 spaces.)

Why did Red Riding
Hood's grandmother
look so strange to her?

(Move 3 spaces.)

**Question**

**Question**

**Question**

**Question**

**Question**

**Question**

**Question**

**Question**

98

The spiteful eighth fairy has cast a spell on you. Go back four spaces.

There was a pea under your mattress and you did not sleep well. Move back two spaces.

Cinderella's fairy godmother helps you. Move ahead two spaces.

The seven dwarfs help you escape from the evil queen. Move ahead three spaces.

The little match girl needs your help. Move back three spaces.

You found a bag of gold. Move ahead two spaces.

You prick your finger on a spindle. Move back two spaces.

The giant caught you. Move back three spaces.

99

**Chance**

**Chance**

**Chance**

**Chance**

**Chance**

**Chance**

**Chance**

**Chance**

100

You can't remember the little man's name. Move back two spaces.

An evil witch cast a spell on you. Go back to Start.

Someone bought a box of matches from you. Move ahead two spaces.

You found a magic wand. Move ahead four spaces.

You found your way home from the forest. Move ahead two spaces.

You got lost in the castle. Move back two spaces.

You lost your favorite broom. Move back three spaces.

You stop to talk to the wolf. Move back 4 spaces.

**Chance**

**Chance**

**Chance**

**Chance**

**Chance**

**Chance**

**Chance**

**Chance**

102

**Cinderella**

**Little Red Riding Hood**

**Rumpelstiltskin**

**Hansel**

**Fairy Godmother**

**Joringel**

103

# Bibliography

Andersen, Hans Christian. *The Little Match Girl.* Boston: Houghton Mifflin Company, 1968.

_____. *The Princess and the Pea.* New York: Seabury Press, 1978.

Disney, Walt. *Snow White and the Seven Dwarfs*, adapted from the work by the Brothers Grimm. New York: Gallery Books, W.H. Smith Publishers, Inc., 1986.

Grimm, The Brothers [Jakob and Wilhelm]. *Hansel and Gretel.* In *Grimms' Fairy Tales,* translated by Mrs. E.V. Lucas, Lucy Crane and Marian Edwardes. New York: Grosset & Dunlop, 1945.

_____. *Jorinda and Joringel.* In *Grimms' Fairy Tales,* translated by Mrs. E.V. Lucas, Lucy Crane and Marian Edwardes. New York: Grosset & Dunlop, 1945.

_____. *Little Red Riding Hood.* New York: Harcourt, Brace & World, Inc., 1968.

_____. *Red Riding Hood.* In *Grimms' Fairy Tales,* translated by Mrs. E.V. Lucas, Lucy Crane and Marian Edwardes. New York: Grosset & Dunlop, 1945.

_____. *Rumpelstitlskin.* In *Grimms' Fairy Tales,* translated by Mrs. E.V. Lucas, Lucy Crane and Marian Edwardes. New York: Grosset & Dunlop, 1945.

_____. *Snow-White and the Seven Dwarfs.* In *Grimms' Fairy Tales,* translated by Mrs. E.V. Lucas, Lucy Crane and Marian Edwardes. New York: Grosset & Dunlop, 1945.

*Jack and the Beanstalk.* In *Famous Fairy Tales.* New York: Wonder Books, 1949.

Perrault, Charles. *Cinderella.* In *Perrault's Complete Fairy Tales,* translated by A.E. Johnson and others. New York: Dodd, Mead & Company, 1961.

_____. *Cinderella, or the Little Glass Slipper,* illustrated by Marcia Brown. New York: Charles Scribner's Sons, 1954.

_____. *Little Red Riding Hood.* In *Perrault's Complete Fairy Tales,* translated by A.E. Johnson and others. New York: Dodd, Mead & Company, 1961.

_____. *The Sleeping Beauty,* translated and illustrated by David Walker. New York: Thomas Y. Crowell Company, 1976.

_____. *The Sleeping Beauty in the Wood.* In *Perrault's Complete Fairy Tales,* translated by A.E. Johnson and others. New York: Dodd, Mead & Company, 1961.

Note: Many different versions of these tales exist. Although similar, they *do* vary in detail.